How to Make a Bird Feeder

D0106880

Liyala Tuckfield
Photographs by Malcolm Cross

Pine Cone Bird Feeder

To make your own bird feeder you will need:

a pine cone

a ball of string

scissors

a teaspoon

a plate

peanut butter

birdseed

a dish

Step 1

Cut the string.
It needs to be as
long as your arm.

Step 2

Tie one end to the top
of your pine cone.

Step 3

Put peanut butter
on your pine cone.

Step 4

Put the birdseed
in a big dish.

Step 5

Roll your pine cone
in the birdseed.

Step 6

Now, tie your pine cone to a tree.

Here come the birds!